A Piece of Home

Jeri Watts

illustrated by Hyewon Yum

CANDLEWICK PRESS

In Korea, my grandmother was a wise and wonderful teacher.
When students bowed, she held her shoulders erect,
but her eyes sparkled.

Even at home, my grandmother could find the extraordinary held within the ordinary. Like how she coaxed her mugunghwa shrubs to blossom into tanshim flowers, revealing their bright red centers.

In Korea, I was ordinary.
A regular boy, playing and laughing and bossing
my little sister, Se Ra.
I was not extraordinary, not different.
I was just me, like so many others.

In Korea, my father, who always did the right thing,
who always did what was expected, surprised us all.
He accepted a position at a law school in West Virginia.

"Who would expect West Virginia?" He laughed, and
so did my mother. I did not.

In swift movements and rapid time, I found my
world packed into three boxes and one suitcase.

Crated,

nailed,

and mailed

to a house
I'd never seen.

In West Virginia, my grandmother stays at home,
and she does not hold her shoulders erect
and her eyes don't gleam — not at all.

In West Virginia, I am not ordinary — I am different.

My eyes are not big and round like everyone else's.
And my hair does not tumble in thick curls or make
a golden halo around my head.

My new classmates smile and talk, but it is sharp noise.
Their names sit like stones on my tongue: Steve. Tom.

Here there are mountains, like in Korea, but the sky seems smaller and darker. I miss the lights of our city. The dark here is so black, at night I touch my eyes to make sure they are open.

But when the pale moon is full and round,
it looks like my face — and a little like the
face of the woman who is now my teacher.

My teacher is nice. She tries to help. She speaks
s-l-o-w-l-y, as if I am stupid — lips snapping over
sounds my mouth will not make.

I try to say I don't want to be here. She nods a lot and smiles but she knows that I do not understand. And I know she does not understand.

Se Ra also does not understand.

She bites and kicks and even spits on her teacher.

My grandmother cries and tries to tell the teacher she is sorry.

Then my father talks to the school in his flawless English. It is decided that my grandmother will go to school with my sister. To give her a bit of ordinary.

She is having a hard time adjusting.

But I have no help.

I wish I were little enough or brave enough to bite and kick and spit.

Days become weeks, and weeks become months.
I learn "Bathroom" and "Please." I am surprised that
I can form words that make their meaning clear,
though they still feel like stones, heavy in my mouth.

They work, though.
"Play with me," like in Korea.
"Pass it back," like in Korea.

Grandmother is learning, too, along with Se Ra. At dinner she tells us about the other children in Se Ra's class and about their young teacher, newly engaged, who helps my grandmother with English at naptime. And my grandmother, with halting words, gives her advice.

One day, Steve says, "Hee Jun, come over."
My first visit to a friend. In his yard, I discover a
red-centered blossom.

"Mugunghwa," I say.
"Rose of Sharon," Steve says.
"It's mugunghwa in Korea," I say.
"It's rose of Sharon here," Steve says.

When I leave, Steve's mother gives me mugunghwa
blossoms and a tender shoot to take home.

"A piece of heaven," Grandmother says.
"A piece of home."

My grandmother plants the shoot, and at the end of the summer, she takes one of the mugunghwa blossoms and sews it onto the wedding dress of her teacher friend, like our family does in Korea. And I can say, "Steve, come over," light like a bubble on my tongue.
And that is ordinary in our new home.

For my grandson Silas, who is always
a big piece of my home, now and forever
J. W.

For Sungjin
H. Y.

First edition 2016

Library of Congress Catalog Card Number 2015934766
ISBN 978-0-7636-6971-3

16 17 18 19 20 21 CCP 10 9 8 7 6 5 4 3 2 1

Printed in Shenzhen, Guangdong, China

This book was typeset in Priori Sans.
The illustrations were done in watercolor.

Candlewick Press
99 Dover Street
Somerville, Massachusetts 02144

visit us at www.candlewick.com